# Baby's Song

Dori Chaconas     Illustrated by Deborah Perez-Stable

# Baby's Song

First Edition
Published by Abingdon Press

**ISBN 978-0-687-49254-1**

08 09 10 11 12 13 14 15 16 17—10 9 8 7 6 5 4 3 2 1

Printed in China

FOR MY MOM AND DAD,
who gave me all the songs

Dori Chaconas

Remembering Nana and Pop and their Shirley Jean. They sang baby's songs for me.
"Like a feather we'll fly over earth and sky. Over mist, over moor, over heather..."

For My Four and George. You still give me reason to sing.
"Be joyful always; pray continually; give thanks in all circumstances,
for this is God's will for you in Christ Jesus." 1 Thessalonians 5:16-18

Thanking Sophia, Roberta, and little Scooter Pie.

Deborah Perez-Stable

Baby, see the paper kite

Chase a springtime breeze!

Send it flying to the sky,

High above the trees.

Swoop-a-loopa!  Swoop-a-loopa!

Sail!  Sail!  Sail!

God has filled the sky with wind.

See the dancing tail!

Baby, look!  An apple tree

Blooming in the spring.

Here's a strong and sturdy branch.

I'll hang a little swing.

To and fro!  Up you go!

High!  High!  High!

God has made the trees so you can

Kick up at the sky.

Baby, come with Momma

To the summertime parade!

Watch the clowns and marching bands.

Sip some lemonade.

Toot-a-tootle!  Toot-a-tootle!

Rum-tum-tum!

God has blessed the earth with song,

So play your little drum!

Baby, ride the wagon
To the salty summer sea.
We will leave your shoes at home
So toes can wiggle free!
Splash-a-kicky!  Splash-a-kicky!
Splish!  Splish!  Splish!
God has made the ocean waves
For my little fish.

Baby, walk with Momma
Where the asters are in flower.
Pack an autumn picnic lunch
And share a sunny hour.
Pick-a-posy!  Pink and rosy!
Yellow, blue, red!
God has made the flowers grow
To crown my baby's head.

Baby, ride a pony
At the Autumn Harvest Fair!
Buy a bag of sugar lumps
For all the horses there.
Clip-a-cloppa!  Clip-a-cloppa!
Ride!  Ride!  Ride!
God has made the pretty horses,
Prancing side by side.

Baby, see the winter snow,

Swirling all around,

Covering the house and gate,

Blanketing the ground.

Roll a snowball!  Make a snowman!

Pat!  Pat!  Pat!

God has made the lacy snow

That decorates your hat.

Baby, on this frosty night
When winter chills the air,
Come and sit with Momma
In the wicker rocking chair.
Rock-a-baby!  Rock-a-baby!
All night long.
God has given you to me!
And so I sing this song.

Thank you for the winter snow.

Thank you for May showers.

Thank you for the prancing horses.

Thank you for the flowers.

Thank you for the music.

Thank you for the sun.

But most of all

I thank you, Lord,

For this little one.

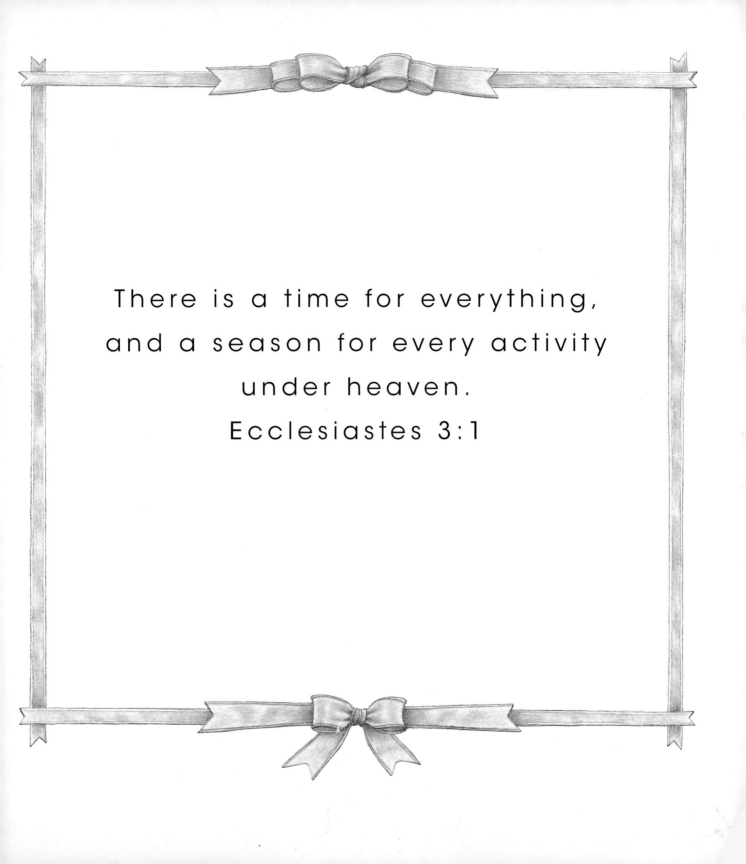

There is a time for everything,
and a season for every activity
under heaven.
Ecclesiastes 3:1